JUST

D.I.V.E

Remove Fear and Shift Your Life from Potential to Greatness

By

Dennis Carter, Jr.

DREAM. IDENTIFY. VISUALIZE. EXECUTE

CONTENTS

DREAM. IDENTIFY. VISUALIZE. EXECUTE

DREAM. IDENTIFY. VISUALIZE. EXECUTE

DEDICATION

To my incredible and supportive wife, Stacy Carter, you are a phenomenal person. The depth of love you possess for God, our son, and I is indescribable. Since 2002, you have been the best woman a man could ever ask for in life. Proverbs 31 wife, you are! You have been the mid-wife of my life and pushed me harder than I could imagine. You have never allowed me to short-change who I am. You saw in me what I did not see in myself. I am forever grateful for you. Until the Lord takes my breath, I promise to be the man of your dreams and give you all that you desire. I love you, beautiful.

To my amazing and incredible son, Dennis Carter III, I love you beyond words. I am so honored that God entrusted your mom and I to have you. I pray that you will grow up to become the pilot that you desire to be. I also pray that you will become a man of valor, humility, and God. I want to leave you with this scripture **(Ephesians 6:10-11)** my father left me before he transitioned to be with the Lord. This scripture has shaped me into the man I am today. Love the Lord with all your heart, and He will direct your path. Until my last breath, I love you immeasurably.

DREAM. IDENTIFY. VISUALIZE. EXECUTE

ACKNOWLEDGEMENT

To my father, the late Prophet Dennis Carter, Sr., and mother, Priscilla Jackson, I love you both. Pops, with tears in my eyes, I miss you so much. Thank you for being a godly example of a man for me. During your time on earth, you have taught me so much about life and ministry. Every time things got hard; your life has shown me another side to a trying season. I hope you are proud of the man I have become and continue to be. See you in Heaven. I love you, Pops!

Mom, I know you are reading this with tears of joy. I love you so much. You are a caring and supportive mother. Thank you for your beautiful heart. I would never ask God for another mother! You have been there for me in ways that I could not imagine. In addition, my sisters and I couldn't thank you enough for your "Nana duties, LOL." The love you have for your grandchildren is immeasurable. You are leaving a piece of your love within them. I pray that you are proud of the man I have become and continue to be. FYI, I am still waiting for my favorite cube steak dinner. Love you, mom. I appreciate and honor you.

To my sisters, Rebecca Carter and De'Breka Gonder. I love you both so much. Thank you for always supporting me and my life endeavors, from business to ministry. You both are incredible in every way. I appreciate all the honest feedback you both have given me while writing this book. I pray you both continue to maximize your life to the fullest and acquire all that your heart's desire. Remember, the cycle is BROKEN; now live life poured out!

My family (grandparents Robert Jackson, Sr., the late Carolyn Jackson, the late Ezelda and Peter Carter, to all my aunts, uncles, cousins, nieces, and nephews), I love you all so much. Thank you all for supporting me. I am forever grateful for the role each of you have in my life. Only God knew that I needed such a hilarious, spiritual, ambitious, and connected family. He has predestined each of us for greatness. Let us leave our impression here on earth and chase after every dream we have. Do not give up until you achieve them. I love you all endlessly.

To my in-laws (my awesome, loving parents, Russell and Belinda Moorman, Angelina Singleton, to my brother and sister, Russell and Shard'e, my grandmother, aunts, uncles, cousins, niece, and nephews), I love you all so much. Thank you for trusting me with Stacy's heart and loving me like family. Each of you hold a special place in

DREAM. IDENTIFY. VISUALIZE. EXECUTE

my heart. I pray you all maximize life to the fullest. Love God with all your heart and trust Him through the process. I love you all and cannot wait until the next gathering!

Lastly, I want to thank all my friends. I am not naming anyone because I know I will forget someone. LOL! I love you all, and I am grateful for the role you all play in my life. The great memories we share are priceless. I cannot wait to celebrate with you all. Continue to seek God, and He will continue to add to you. Live life that is pleasing to Him. Make an impact in the lives of others. I love you all; do not stop until you see what you have said.

HOW TO MAXIMIZE DURING YOUR READING TIME

Every dreamer's goal is to see their purpose, dreams, and goals manifest to become tangible. I believe that you will read this book and not place it on the shelf. I speak something purposeful, something meaningful is within you, and it is waiting to come out! This book is an investment towards your purpose and future endeavors. I want you to not only read this book, but also to follow the **"JUST D.I.V.E"** strategy for success. To maximize your reading time, you should focus on:

- Having an open mindset to gather information and to gain understanding and new insight.
- Highlighting important areas that stand out to you to retain the information!
- Writing down your thoughts and what you have learned at the end of each chapter. Become a student!
- Executing what you have learned. Do not waste any time! Take it one step at a time.

DREAM. IDENTIFY. VISUALIZE. EXECUTE

INTRODUCTION

This book was birthed through a prophetic prayer conference, where I was invited as a guest speaker. This conference was hosted by Pastors Kevin and Berneka Alleyne from Lehigh Acres, FL. I was assigned to speak about "New Strategies and Tools for Success." This was a virtual conference at the height of the pandemic. However, it was a very impactful conference. While preparing to speak, God gave me the message, "**JUST D.I.V.E.**" I knew it was an important, relevant message. Initially, I did not have clarity on where God was taking it. Though, I sensed He would give me an opportunity to create more beyond this message.

After the conference, I was humbled by the number of testimonies I received. I jokingly said I wanted to write a book and go more in-depth with my message. I always desired to host workshops and seminars to empower others. I began to feel God place a fire in me to proceed, so I stated I wanted to create a strategy book. Pastor Berneka immediately challenged me to set a date and prepare for it. During the process, I realized this assignment was speaking life to stagnated areas and things that were lying dormant. I had the liberty to think about what I desired to do with it.

DREAM. IDENTIFY. VISUALIZE. EXECUTE

I understood that **"JUST D.I.V.E"** was not only for myself; it was for the masses. God gave me this idea to help other people strategize to accomplish their dreams, goals, and purpose. With this book, people can break cycles in their lives, increase their belief measures, and pursue what they desire to acquire. Social, mental, emotional, spiritual, and financial cycles have created barriers for many people. I believe it has held the masses captive far too long and prevented them from executing their life endeavors. These obstacles have caused people to create mental blocks and self-denial. Life circumstances and dream killers have paralyzed many people's potential and momentum to become greater.

If I reflect on my life, I can relate to the days of facing obstacles and giants. I refused to allow the words and actions of others to penetrate my spirit. I recognized that I had the choice to come in agreement with it or to reject it. I had the power to control my destiny, my future, and my life. I took away the opportunity for people to be in the driver's seat or become the captain of my purpose, dreams, and goals. When they said no, I said **Go, "JUST D.I.V.E!"**

The measure of self-belief is not enough to manifest what is required to build towards your vision. You must get to the place where you work hard to obtain

DREAM. IDENTIFY. VISUALIZE. EXECUTE

what you desire. Sometimes, we allow life situations and people to alter our thoughts and actions. As a result, the attempt to try is not even an option! It is not always people or things that are holding us back. Sometimes, it is ourselves that can become the mountain, the wall, and the stumbling block. It is easy to place the cause of your downfall and delay on others. Some may question why do people do this? It is because many people feel better covering their mishaps and mistakes rather than exposing them. We speak delays and death by our very own speech pattern. It does not all derive from the outside world and those who are close to us.

Find a person or thing that inspires and motivates you to seek after what is waiting for you. Whatever you desire to accomplish, you can do it! Whether you may be pursuing entrepreneurial opportunities, attending college, purchasing real estate, seeking promotions, or starting a ministry assignment, you can do it.

If I were to ask you two questions, it would be:

1. Can you imagine how life would be if you lived out your purpose, dreams, and goals?
2. If you found the strategy to shift your pain into purpose, remove fear, and gain forward momentum, would you initiate and maximize on the opportunity?

DREAM. IDENTIFY. VISUALIZE. EXECUTE

If yes, **what is stopping you**?

This book will give you the strategies and tools you need to pursue it. Work it by using your God-given gifts, talents, and abilities that you possess. You have the capacity to do it! Growing up, one of my favorite events to watch was and still is "the Olympics." I loved watching the diving competition. I have learned that a diver's score is based upon four elements: **approach, take-off, execution, and entry** into the water. I wanted to correlate the essence of diving into your purpose, dreams, and goals with the techniques of a diver. I wanted this book to be the birthing piece to inspire and empower others in every area of their lives. As you read, you will begin to see how a diver and a dreamer harmonize together to give you another perspective for success. If you apply this strategy to your life, nothing can hold you back from prospering. **"JUST D.I.V.E!"**

> Dream (Approach)
> Identify (Take-off)
> Visualize (Execution)
> Execute (Entry)

DREAM. IDENTIFY. VISUALIZE. EXECUTE

DREAM

——— APPROACH **———**

Take delight in the LORD, and he will give you the desires of your heart~ **Psalm 37:4**

"Success is not measured on how much you have acquired; however, it is measured on how many people are better off because you lived and chased after your dream!" ~**Anonymous**

DREAMING HAS NO LIMITATIONS

You may be questioning how a diver can truly connect with you achieving something in your life? I'm a person that emphasizes different aspects and perspectives of everything. This allows me to paint the picture and explain the narrative more effectively. Before I speak about the dream phase, you will see precisely why I chose a diver to pull this all together. Exploring the concepts and components of a diver, it will show that it requires extensive training and planning.

First, you must perfect your **identity** as a diver, enhance your diving **techniques**, then find **effective methods** to increase your success rate. Please be aware; I am not referring to the casual weekend swimmer. I am speaking of someone who makes the necessary **sacrifices** and does whatever it takes to become a top-notch diver. Before initiating to jump, they are scored on their **approach**. This involves the number of steps taken to get to the end of the diving board and arm placement to transition to the take-off phase. The approach must be very smooth and precise to have a great take-off. If the diver's arms are flaring unsynchronized, then it will be very shabby.

DREAM. IDENTIFY. VISUALIZE. EXECUTE

This concept compares to a dreamer. Dream building is one of the most important phases to execute your life endeavors and purpose. It is common for many people to be unaware of what they desire to do or be. As a result, it is difficult to make it come to reality. While some may need to discover what they like to accomplish, others do not have it on their minds. If you can relate, take the time to determine or rediscover what you wish to attain. The things you have a passion for could identify your purpose, skill, or gift. What you love to do could turn into a thriving business. I want you to ask yourself:

- What did God purpose for me to do?
- What are my strengths and passion?
- What gives me fulfillment and makes me feel complete?
- What would I do even if it did not yield a profit?
- Where do I see myself in 1-3 years? How about 5-10 years?
- What do I desire to have in life?
- What do I desire that I cannot stop thinking about every day?

These are a few questions to guide you along the way. People can live a limited and unfulfilled life when they forsake what they love or are purposed to do. Whether it is related to business, college, marriage, ministry, health,

DREAM. IDENTIFY. VISUALIZE. EXECUTE

or financial wealth, you must be aware of it and live for it. Find practical ways to get started and pursue them! Let us dive into this strategy to find ways to be effective. When you aspire to be successful, extensive preparation and planning is required. You cannot wake up and believe it would not involve you putting in the effort. A detailed plan is necessary to follow through for your desired result.

Many can relate to going forth with a dream and lack the proper steps to take. Some can confirm failing to identify the critical areas of finding strategies and tools and finding ways to increase their success. It is not wise to be so quick to get to the take-off phase. Challenges will arise when building a dream or vision that you do not believe in wholeheartedly. The more you trust, the more you create self-confidence and effort to produce what you desire. This book is not for the unintentional, casual daydreamer. It is purposed for those who are seeking something better, something greater. Whether you need resources or that push to go forth, the **"JUST D.I.V.E"** strategy will give you greater insight.

DREAM. IDENTIFY. VISUALIZE. EXECUTE

PSYCHOLOGY OF A DREAMER

As you dream, it is beneficial to understand the mind of the dreamer! I want you to answer a few questions by being authentic and transparent. You will be able to recognize and clarify your dream and the size of it. It will reveal if you need to expand your mind or remove selfish gains from it. As you answer them, check your ambition and dedication level. The results will determine if you desire to make your dreams **tangible** or **remain stored** in your head as a wish. I like to refer to these questions as the dream identifiers.

Here are **seven dream identifiers**:

1. Have you identified your dreams and goals?
2. How dedicated are you to self-investing and remaining focused on the process?
3. Can you live without seeing your purpose and life endeavors manifesting?
4. How do you handle opposition or challenges?
5. Are you self-motivated, or do you need an accountability partner to push you continually?
6. How can others benefit from you chasing and accomplishing your dreams and goals?
7. Are you ready to start the **"JUST D.I.V.E."** strategy, or do you need more time?

DREAM. IDENTIFY. VISUALIZE. EXECUTE

To fulfill a purpose, dream, or goal, you must realize it initiates as a seed in your mind. Just as in nature, it needs a conducive environment to manifest and mature. What dwells within you requires an environment that protects, feeds, and cultivates your potential. Have you created a conducive environment to manifest growth in your life? If you have not, you need to plow and fertilize your mental garden. You are responsible for what is in it. Protect your mind from the mental weeds that try to choke out the fruit from your garden. You must be on guard and protect what God has given you!

Do not allow anyone to drop negative seeds in your mind. Protect your mental aspect at all costs. This includes your family and friends! Just remember that you cannot have a penthouse dream with a toolshed mentality. Uproot it, so it does not suffocate your potential. You would be amazed at what you can produce if you would feed the seed. I have a saying that says, "If you can find the seed that God placed on the inside of you, you would be amazed at what you can become." Do not spend your life feeding and watering the seed in another person's garden. Your seed is deserving of nourishment as well.

DREAM. IDENTIFY. VISUALIZE. EXECUTE

There is nothing in this world that is produced or made without it. Let us use fruit as an example. If you plant an apple seed, the root will begin to mature. You would need to cut the tree down in order for the seeds to stop producing fruit. The giving potential of that apple seed is limitless. Let me use another example. Did you know the blueprint of a physical building is birthed from the seed of a thought? Before someone created the structure, it was initiated as an idea or a seed. Once it is planted or placed in your mind, manifestation can begin. It is evident that it is the birthing place for greatness.

This same perspective applies to the dreamer. Once you find and feed the seed of greatness that is within you, you will be unstoppable. Your passion, your dream, your vision, and your purpose will continue to develop and produce never-ending fruit in your life. The more you sow, the more you will yield your desired results. What if other people could benefit from the value that's within you? As your seed develops, you will need to continue to preserve your mental maintenance. Become intentional with managing your thoughts and actions. An unguarded mind will lead to fruitless seasons.

DREAM. IDENTIFY. VISUALIZE. EXECUTE

Do you realize that your thinking matters? It really does matter! It shapes who you are and who you will become. Where you are in life is a consistent flow of your thought patterns. This is something you knowingly or unknowingly adapt to or become conditioned over time. I understand that life happens, and unfortunate circumstances can and will arise. However, the way you control and deal with the issue **determines the fruit**. You cannot allow the difficulties of life to shut down your dream and mental tank. If you lose your ability to create and think yourself out of a situation, you will sever your tree to produce tangible results.

With the dreamer's outlook, let us explore a biblical perspective. I am a believer of the Word of God. Whether one agrees with the Bible or not, we can agree that it is saturated with proven principles to encourage, enlighten, and empower people. I recommend that everyone include biblical principles in their strategy for success. It will undoubtedly help you to materialize and mobilize what you desire to do or be. **Proverbs 23:7** says, "for as a man thinketh in his heart, so is he." Stop and think about that for a minute!" What you consistently think about will begin to affect you.

DREAM. IDENTIFY. VISUALIZE. EXECUTE

Determine your consistent thought pattern. If it is not in alignment with the life you desire, you must **change it**! Everything you wish for in life is on the other side of your thoughts. Change your mindset to shift your season! Depending on where you currently are, I want you to become bold and yell out, "**I've changed my mind**." Why do I want you to do this? By taking that step of liberty, you will make a purposeful declaration to yourself. Anyone in your vicinity will know that your **new day** is activating now. It is here! No longer will you dwell on things you cannot control—no more excuses for why you are not where you want to be in life.

Today, you will change your language and speak possibilities and potential over your life. Do you realize that you have just severed the head of your yesterday and the negative root that was in your mind? **Shift** to who you need to become or what you need to do to reach what you desire to accomplish! I want to look at another perspective from that same verse. By meditating on the scripture, it expresses that your head and heart are **directly** connected. Did you know that your brain is only 12 to 18 inches away from your heart? This is a short distance away in physical nature, yet it carries many miles. This measurement can produce a lifetime of value when it is maximized to the fullest potential. How are you using your distance? Does it consist of misery, pain, and regret?

DREAM. IDENTIFY. VISUALIZE. EXECUTE

Or, does it consist of you pursuing and striving for achievement, success, and fulfillment in your life?

You have the power and ability to control the outcome. If you do not take control or get in the captain seat of your journey, life's complications will. This scripture also tells me that my heart has a mind. The mind in my heart and the mind in my head **must** speak the same language for success to be birthed and manifested. Have you ever attempted to successfully have a conversation with someone of a different foundation than you? Or, maybe that person spoke another language that you are not fluent in or even recognized? It would be difficult to have an even exchange of a simple conversation. It is not because either party is unwilling to communicate. It merely results from having no source of a recognizable connection or an understanding between the two. When there is no connection, there is no success in any capacity.

The Bible says in **Amos 3:3,** "Can two walk together, except they be agreed"? It shows that your heart and mind must walk together simultaneously to reach what you desire to see. There must be an agreement. Once they initiate to speak different languages, it becomes foreign to each other, the ambition level weakens, and frustration takes residence. It will cause you to second-

DREAM. IDENTIFY. VISUALIZE. EXECUTE

guess yourself. Settling will begin to creep in to confuse and stagnate your mind.

Your head and mind can attain more, but your heart is not in the same environment. The great thing is that you desire more but lack the drive you need to push yourself. Perhaps what is in your heart can be determined, but not in your mind. It is parallel to you being in the driver's seat with your foot on the gas in either setting. Yet, the car is in neutral. At this point, you are wasting time and energy. When they are not synchronized, you will waste years speaking about what you will do but never act on it. In reality, society would classify these types of people as talkers. If you can relate, change the narrative. Start working on your purpose, dreams, and goals that you have set out for yourself. Become focused and intentionally put your heart and mind on the same path.

Never commit to anything without the two participating together. You need them to agree to create useful energy and efforts. Once your commitment is established and settled, you will be able to pursue them and not give up. The world will begin to see that your seed of greatness truly lies within your heart. It would become more evident that you are a doer and not a talker. To create momentum, your mind must be on one accord with your heart. Let us briefly discuss the power of

DREAM. IDENTIFY. VISUALIZE. EXECUTE

influence. What is it exactly? It is the power of a person or thing having the ability to positively or negatively impact someone else. The person who has both on one accord is not easily persuaded. They are planted and rooted in their plan and decision. On the other hand, someone who is not on one accord will be easily shaken and shifted mentally. Their plans and desires will always be tampered with, and it will never come forth to be tangible.

Never set a goal or pursue anything based upon the desires of someone else. It must be a personal commitment to yourself to be motivated to move. This dream must be so touching that you cannot live without it. It should be beyond monetary benefits and public recognition. Those are some of the necessities to maintain a constant flow of healthy habits, thoughts, and speech patterns. **Psalms 20:4** encourages us with this uplifting scripture. It says, "May He give you the desires of your heart and make all your plans succeed." This tells us what God will do for us. He will make everything that we desire accessible to us. While pursuing your purpose, dreams, and goals, you must be in alignment with God's will for your life. Never chase anything outside of your destiny. You should always use wisdom and direction. It will allow you to have a seamless journey.

SPEECH PATTERNS OF A DREAMER

"A good man brings good things out of the good stored up in his heart, and an evil man brings evil things out of the evil stored up in his heart. For the mouth speaks what the heart is full of," says **Luke 6:45**. If your heart is full of dreams, possibilities, and accomplishments, then your mouth has no choice but to speak what is within it. Ironically, this works in reverse. If your heart is full of fear, doubt, and what-ifs, then your mouth has no choice but to speak that which is in it.

Once they march to the same beat, your mouth has no choice but to articulate what is in your heart. How you speak is a direct correlation of your thoughts, beliefs, and emotions. Never allow anyone or anything to disrupt your speaking patterns. Remain in harmony, so you can articulate and speak your next! Your purpose, dreams, and goals are waiting for your words to pump life into them.

Proverbs 18:21 declares that "life and death are in the power of the tongue, and those who love it will eat its fruit." Who we are as a person is a consistent series of our thoughts and words that have patterned us to act and think as we do. Consider that for a moment. You are what is in your mind and what comes out of your mouth.

DREAM. IDENTIFY. VISUALIZE. EXECUTE

That is very powerful! If someone wanted to become a doctor, they would submerge their thoughts and energy in resources concerning the medical field. They will then start to attract new information, mentors, and opportunities beyond their speaking pattern and focus in their lives. If you are not in agreement with what is on your plate, **change** what is in your heart so that your mouth can articulate your breakthrough and a new season.

It is impossible to obtain success without a healthy speech pattern that aligns with your vision. It gives it life. How is this possible? Your language arrangement creates your daily affirmations. Say them every day to yourself out loud to program your subconscious mind to respond to your speaking pattern. It is what many would call "commanding your day." You need to take authority over your day! When this happens, you are intentionally taking daily steps to align your thoughts and speech pattern for success. You have the power or control to change any situation by speaking what you want. You can change the trajectory of your life. The act of thinking optimistically is not strong enough to adjust to an atmosphere. However, when you start to express what you feel and believe, you will begin to shift your climate. Many are not familiar or acquainted with this term for several reasons. However, some are accustomed to this phrase yet fail to practice it.

DREAM. IDENTIFY. VISUALIZE. EXECUTE

I want you to become more intentional with taking control of your day. Not only should your purpose, dreams, and goals excite you, but your daily affirmations should fire you up and keep you lifted! Please take the time to implement this and practice affirming it to yourself. Practice a short speech exercise loudly and boldly: "I am a winner, bold, and sharp. I am confident and intelligent. I'm resilient. I am excited, a positive thinker, and speaker. My day is always prosperous, and I attract influential people in my life. I am passionate, and I'm turning my dreams into reality! It is manifesting. I am blessed to be a blessing. I am the Moses of my family. I will not stop pursuing my dreams and goals. There is a fighter in me, and I will not stop swinging until the bell rings. My work ethic is unbeatable, and I am laser focused. Winning is second nature to me. Are you fired up yet?

You must mentally and vocally reject and realign any thought that comes against your vision. Do not allow any negativity to dwell too long and take root. It will choke out the purpose, dreams, and goals you have set out for yourself. Recognize when something comes against it. Immediately, you must declare, "I do not accept this thought. You will not take residence and reside in my mind because it is in direct alignment with my destiny." Once you begin to speak these affirmations, everything

DREAM. IDENTIFY. VISUALIZE. EXECUTE

will come under the submission of your new thought process and belief. You will then notice that your atmosphere will shift into your everyday speech and mental pattern. It is necessary and vital on every level! Your mind should only focus on one thing at a time. By not allowing those negative thoughts to linger, it will begin to reset your mind.

You attract what is in your mind and what comes out of your mouth. The power of attraction is valuable and necessary for your life endeavors because they are the doors to your future. The connection brings a quality level of advisors, mentors, association, new information, and opportunities to you that would not be the norm in your life. It is the fuel that keeps you moving from one level to the next. In conjunction, this principle applies in the negative aspect as well. You will attract undesirable things and people in your life if you begin to speak and think about the wrong things. Once your words leave your mouth, you may not be able to reclaim them. Your heart automatically starts to seek for what you spoke to manifest them. Be careful of what you speak! It could be the very thing that is preventing you from progressing to your best season! Your words are powerful!

DREAM. IDENTIFY. VISUALIZE. EXECUTE

As you use them in the right context, you will begin to see a shift become present in your life. Every great thing encounters opposition to test the strength and validity of it. It is the testing, resistance, stumbling blocks, disagreement, and frustration towards your purpose, dreams, and goals. There are things and people that create the negative and cause you to quit! If you fold under pressure, you will never see what your potential could have yielded you. Can you stand the test? Can you deal with pressure coming against it?

You must begin to take note of what's stopping you from accomplishing or initiating them. If you have positioned yourself to learn, progress, and build, then you are in the right spot. Do not move from that place! Focus on those affirmations if you did not start! It may look or feel foreign to you now, but you will see the results. Focus on affirming to yourself one day at a time! If you are currently encouraging yourself, I commend you! It definitely works! Dive into those positive words and wait for it.

EMOTIONS OF A DREAMER

Now that you understand the dreamer's psychology and speech pattern, it is time to fuel the rocket. You will

DREAM. IDENTIFY. VISUALIZE. EXECUTE

learn how to balance your emotions effectively. One of the greatest mental tools that you possess is your mind. Internal and external influences can cause quick emotional reactions. It is the control panel for your feelings when dream building or setting goals. It helps your mind to decipher and create effectively. Your imagination can take you places that your physical body has not been.

Have you ever seen a child imaginatively play by themselves or with another child? They would have an entire adventure within their play space. They would create conversations, places, people, feelings, or food. The world they live in would become so real to them until they asked a parent to participate. Imagine if you could take all the limitations off your mind and allow yourself to envision yourself as a youth again. The world and the results that you could manifest would be limitless. Once you have created that space of fearless possibilities, invite people to share the experience with you. It would be inevitable for you to have massive growth in your life. How do your emotions control your imagination? It can fuel your creativity and affect your foundation. When feelings are positive, you can create and build with a clear mind. When they are negative, it becomes difficult to envision and create.

DREAM. IDENTIFY. VISUALIZE. EXECUTE

Your success for what you desire to be or do is determined by how you imagine, think, feel, and speak. I want you to take a moment to practice a **quick emotional exercise**: Close your eyes and put your purpose, dreams, and goals in front of your mind. Imagine accomplishing what you desire in a short timeframe, having tangible resources, and how your life would be. Think of the people you could connect with and those who would benefit from your achievement. Now open your eyes and settle your mind. How did it feel to complete your goals and having everything you desire? I want you to take that same scenario and picture yourself not achieving it. Envision yourself quitting and never giving yourself a fair shot. In what way did that make you feel now? That is how powerful your imagination is.

It takes you seconds to feel the results of you obtaining it or not. Your purpose, dreams, and goals should be so meaningful to you until it moves you to act upon them. You would need to create and maintain an effective emotional support system to carry them. This is a method you would have to keep your desires alive. Here are a few ways to connect and support them: Close your eyes and use your imagination to measure where you are and what you need to accomplish them. Continue to remind yourself how it would feel to achieve them by envisioning yourself winning.

DREAM. IDENTIFY. VISUALIZE. EXECUTE

If you can support it effectively, then there is no stopping you. As long as you have a method to fuel it, then quitting is never an option. Have you ever decided to give up on your dreams or quit on yourself? It is necessary to identify and evaluate where you are emotionally and mentally. When you have a healthy mindset, your passion will come to life. A consistent flow of positive support paired with a great mental attitude will increase your drive.

Knowing your why and having a healthy level of passion is what separates you from the rest. Your why gives you something to fight for and gives you meaning for why you are doing it. It challenges your current level of comfortability and makes you dig deeper. It will cause you to break out of those comfort zones and cycles. Your why is what drives you and keeps you creating forward momentum. Being passionate about what you love or purposed to do will cause you to become very contagious. Everyone will be able to see your determination and drive. You will start to attract more things and like-minded people into your life.

While one's desire may cause excitement, another person could cause fear that blurs your thinking and belief. What do I mean by this? Some people have passion but battle with fear. This conflict will have people

DREAM. IDENTIFY. VISUALIZE. EXECUTE

asking themselves if they have what it takes, will it work, who would not accept it, and who would support it. Anxiety will cause you to stunt your growth and never see your purpose, dreams, and goals come to past. Fear is only a distraction! Say that to yourself; **FEAR IS ONLY A DISTRACTION!** Many use this acronym, which says, Fear is "False Evidence Appearing Real."

It heightens the negative possibilities, which brings false information that appears as mirages. These illusions are mental. It presents itself as mountains to cripple your progress and forward momentum. Fear brings attention to your insufficiencies and inabilities to stagnate you. Imagine this as a person. Its' name is called "fear." It would tell you that you are not qualified to be successful because you are not educationally inclined, lack resources, are not good enough, and give this dream up for good! Remember, this is only a deception! It is false information, and this is not who you are! You can do everything that you desire to do. Understand that this mountain or distraction you may be experiencing; you can tackle this head-on! It can be climbed and conquered. This takes courage and effort!

What appears to be holding you back could be the very thing that gives you the stretch you need. After facing this thing called "Fear," you can defeat it! You can stand

DREAM. IDENTIFY. VISUALIZE. EXECUTE

on top of it and shout your victory. "I made it through, and I am ready to continue this route to reach my goal." You have the power to eliminate it or use it for your good. You will either be driven by **fear** or **faith**. When anxiety sets in, what is your reaction? How do you handle the situation? You will either act from a place of stress or a place of passion. Sometimes, it can be a reverse psychology mechanism. You can fear living a life of stunted growth, so you find ways to prosper. You can dread not pursuing your business idea, becoming a new homeowner, or leader you are called to be. As a result, it causes you not to quit. You have to know what is taking residence in your life. Your purpose, dreams, and goals are on the line.

FOCUS OF A DREAMER

It takes a high level of concentrated focus to manifest what you plan to do. Before a diver physically moves any part of their body to perform a dive, they sit and internalize their routine. The focus level of a dreamer has to be that of a diver. Despite the people watching, cheering you on, or those who view you as competition, reframe from putting your focus there. Do not get sidetracked and lose your concentration. Sit, internalize,

DREAM. IDENTIFY. VISUALIZE. EXECUTE

and make your moves! It is just you, your dreams, and goals that should have your attention. It is you against yourself. You are your own competition! Internalize what you need to do, how to mobilize, and how to manage the impact of achieving your set-out task. Focusing on anything long enough will eventually manifest. Never let what your eyes see overpower what your faith sees. If you can concentrate despite the shortcomings, there is no telling what you can accomplish.

Having your purpose, dreams, and goals clearly defined and speaking them into existence will increase your ability to obtain them. Once you learn how to master your cognitive psychology and fuel them with healthy emotions, improving your vision will become easier. There is a phrase that says, "If the dream is big enough, the facts do not matter." When your dream is clearly defined and makes you want to move, lacking financial resources, opportunities, or equipment does not matter. Once you start moving towards your vision, you will begin to work your faith muscle despite not having everything you need. Your strength will build and increase as you continue to believe. Your faith gives you confidence, despite what you see. It will begin to manifest the very tools that you needed from the beginning.

Turn your dreams into your vision and create goals. Before you declare it, be sure to connect with your dreams. If this is not apparent, redefine what they are. Sometimes, the aspiration of other people can influence you. However, this does not mean it is the direction you should take. Be sure it connects to your passion, or it will turn into an obligation or failure. You should be laser focused. Likened of the diver, your approach to take-off must be crisp, organized, and clearly defined before you jump. Preparation is key!

Those who fail to prepare are preparing to fail! Heading to college, purchasing a home, or opening a new business requires homework. Yes, it would be amazing to zoom past the process and head straight to the prize. Would this benefit you or would you appreciate it? Does life really work that way? By staying focused on your life endeavors, it will set you apart. It will determine your speed to accomplish it. The more you are focused, the faster you can reach your goals. Eliminate distractions, create a routine, and persevere. No one will be able to convince you to give up. It will create a drive in you to push harder when others doubt your ability to perform. Set your mind, remove the negativity, protect your mental space, and conquer what you set out to do. You got what it takes.

DREAM. IDENTIFY. VISUALIZE. EXECUTE

DREAM BIBLICAL INSPIRATION

The story of David defeating Goliath **1 Samuel 17:1-54**

I will present all four stages of the **"JUST D.I.V.E"** strategy within David and Goliath's battle and how David achieved victory. In this chapter of the book, I will show you the **D(ream)** aspect of David before he fought.

Reading this story, we understand that Goliath was a part of the Philistine army, who challenged the Israelites. He began to taunt the Israelites until the entire army was terrified of him due to his size. He teased and tested the Israelites for forty days. No one would step up to fight Goliath. One day, Jesse (David's father) asked David to take his three oldest brothers (Eliab, Abinadab, and Shammah) and the commanding officer's food and check on them. David got up the next morning to do as his father requested. He left all the food with the commanding officers and ran to the battle lines to check on his brothers. While speaking with his brothers, Goliath re-challenged the army.

After hearing the giant, they all ran away in terror. "Look at him," they said to each other. Listen to his challenge! King Saul promised to give a big reward to the man who kills him. He will also give him his daughter to marry and will not require his father's family to pay taxes.

David asked the men who were near him, "What will the man get who kills this Philistine and frees Israel from this disgrace?

After all, who is this heathen who defies the army of the living God?" They told him what the reward would be for the man who killed Goliath. He started to (D)ream and internalized the kings' promise. I am sure he had thoughts of how the reward could benefit him and his family. So, he asked the other soldiers that were near him the same thing. Every time he asked, it was the same answer. With so many questions asked, his older brother Eliab became very angry. He told him to go home and stop trying to get a front-row seat to the battle. He did not care about how his brothers felt. He had a dream.

Just as David, you should do the same. When you have a dream, please do not allow anyone or anything to deter your confidence to accomplish it. Even when everyone around you is afraid to conquer their giants, commit to your dream and internalize the benefit. David heard the benefits of defeating Goliath, and it motivated him to act. Take his mindset and listen to what your heart is saying that you can have, do, or become. Be confident in your ability to perform and move with motivation.

KEY POINTS:

- Identify your purpose, dreams, and goals.
- Understand that you are greater than your current place in life.
- Never become complacent with your now.
- Ensure that your heart and mind are in alignment with where you are heading.
- Make your speech patterns support and flow in the same direction as your dreams and goals.
- Use the power of affirmations to attract, motivate, and empower.
- Remove the limitations from your imagination.
- Emotionally envision yourself accomplishing everything you desire.
- Eliminate distractions and remain laser-focused until you have accomplished your vision.

DREAM. IDENTIFY. VISUALIZE. EXECUTE

Take a few minutes to write down the purpose, dreams, or goals you are looking to accomplish.

_____

_____

_____

_____

_____

_____

_____

_____

_____

_____

_____

_____

_____

_____

_____

_____

_____

_____

_____

_____

_____

_____

DREAM. IDENTIFY. VISUALIZE. EXECUTE

IDENTIFY

— TAKE-OFF —

I have considered my ways and have turned my steps to your statutes. I will hasten and not delay to obey your commands.
Psalm 119:59-60

Any dream or goal will wither into a wish if it is unfed! Feed your dreams and goals with passion! ~**Dennis Carter**

DREAM. IDENTIFY. VISUALIZE. EXECUTE

TAKING THE STEPS

After initiating the approach phase of your dive, you can move to the next step called Take-Off. It is when the diver transitions to the end of the board by either a hop or jump. They would take off with one foot and then land on both feet. They would proceed to leave the board, in transition to the next point. They must identify a safe distance for safety precautions. As a dreamer, you must first determine and decipher why you are chasing after your dreams and goals. If you are aware of why you are doing something, then quitting is never an option. Your reason must be so meaningful that you cannot picture life without having it. It should stir up your emotions and bring out the fighter in you.

In comparison to the diver, you must detect how you need to move and decide what is required to obtain it. Before you transition, take the proper steps to accomplish your vision without any delays. By not calculating your next move and recognizing your areas of opportunity can cause significant failure and conflict. I cannot imagine anyone desiring to start their journey to greatness and fail before anything happens. This will result from you neglecting to take the necessary steps to properly identify each move for you to execute a successful "**dive.**"

DREAM. IDENTIFY. VISUALIZE. EXECUTE

Why are you initiating to dive? Why are calculated steps crucial to your success? These are just a few questions that you would need to answer to have an understanding. As you go in the right direction, the closer your results will become more evident. You will begin to discover your strengths, weaknesses, and new opportunities to accomplish your purpose, dreams, and goals. Are you being realistic and authentic? You should ask yourself if they are goals, or are they wishes and wants? Are they specific, or are they all over the place? Can it be defined where you can measure how much work is needed for you to be successful?

Identifying is a very significant factor in accomplishing everything. Everyone's why factor is different. Before you proceed, it is essential to classify why you want to do or be what you desire to achieve. Create an atmosphere that supports and fuels it. Your present environment can either drive or drain your why. If you are frequently around negativity, the impact will become your downfall. It could cause you to lack engagement and smother what is most important. Protect it with everything you have! This is a part of the core of your purpose, dreams, and goals. It will be the support center as you continue to move closer to the things you desire. There will be moments throughout your journey where you will feel that it is easier to give up. I speak against the thoughts of

DREAM. IDENTIFY. VISUALIZE. EXECUTE

giving up! You will stay inspired and keep your feet moving. Protect your core!

WHAT IS THE BIG DEAL?

What is the significance of identifying and becoming one with your dreams and goals? What is the level of significance of you going after them? Can you imagine life filled without dreams, goals, and visions? This would be a meaningless world that lacks possibilities and purpose. God did not design for life to be that way! He has placed something unique and special in every one of us to be utilized and witnessed. He has given us the ability to obtain whatever we desire alongside quality principles and a good work ethic. Dreaming that was initiated from our younger days created excitement and motivation in our lives. Now that we are adults, should we stop? Should we be ashamed to admit it?

Vision does not cease because of your age. It has no age limitations, nor does it have any restrictions. In life, you will have many obstacles that could potentially stagnant or kill your desire to dream or believe. You must measure your confidence. If you evaluated it, what will be the outcome? Your determination plays a significant role

DREAM. IDENTIFY. VISUALIZE. EXECUTE

in how you do things every day. If it was insufficient, you could expect your desires never to be fulfilled or take years to make simple steps to see the manifestation. Sometimes, your passion changes over time. What you desired 5-10 years ago could no longer be valid due to life changes or bigger goals. Ensure that they are current, and your drive intensity will follow.

Recognizing key areas is one of the best ways to bring forth fruit during your process. You should identify what will help you succeed and what will hold you back. The problem initiates when you waste time. As time passes by, you are sitting on your purpose, dreams, and goals. You will watch everyone else win while you cheer them on. Stop sitting on the sidelines, being the professional cheerleader! You will continue to witness them achieving new levels; while you are in the same place being unproductive. You cannot get upset with anyone but yourself. Do not lose sight of your own desires and endeavors.

Have you forgotten about yourself or what God promised you? Be the person you desire to be or do by eliminating what is in the way. Identify those stumbling blocks that are creating the barriers. To produce what you aspire to have, you must say something you never said before and do what you have never done. What do I

DREAM. IDENTIFY. VISUALIZE. EXECUTE

mean by this? Stop speaking against yourself. You express doubt and become reserved. You allow fear to creep in and create a language that is contrary to growth. You want to produce your dreams to reality; yet, you have failed to write your goals down. Can you relate to this? Many have failed to change their mindset and daily routine. Many have failed to invest in themselves and shift their thinking? You are capable of more, and you deserve more! Many can relate, at some point, needing to build self-confidence to fulfill and produce something new. You must unlock and release those God-given gifts, talents, and abilities. Let go and **D.I.V.E!**

Would you believe me if I told you that someone is waiting on you to believe in yourself? What you have, somebody needs it! What you are sitting on could be someone else's solution! What you accomplish could inspire others! What you possess could save the lives of many people! Let me use an example of a person aspiring to be a doctor. From the moment of believing, that is the antidote to becoming a successful doctor. As a result, they become the gateway to saving many people's lives and giving them a second chance at life. You, too, are significantly important.

DREAM. IDENTIFY. VISUALIZE. EXECUTE

If you could only see through the lenses of God to see your potential, it would floor you at your possibilities. Are you aware of how He views you? How do you view yourself? You must elevate your level of thinking and belief. The things that are keeping you mentally, spiritually, financially, or emotionally bound, you must identify it, call it by name, and speak against it! You need a public declaration to yourself and to those who will hold you accountable. This is necessary because it vocalizes and brings recognition to your vision. It expresses to yourself and others that you are on a mission to set yourself apart and working hard to change your life.

Once you have made this public declaration that you are pursuing your dreams and goals, skeptics will start to appear from everywhere. Saying this declaration to the wrong person, you must be emotionally and mentally resilient. The skeptics will attempt to convince you not to proceed and why others have failed at what you are trying to do. You must choose to be a thermostat instead of a thermometer. What does this mean? A thermostat sets and controls the atmosphere while the thermometer measures and adapts to the environment. When people begin to send negative energy your way, you should stand up and readjust the room temperature to guard your dream. You have the power to set and control what affects you and how you respond. Never adapt to

DREAM. IDENTIFY. VISUALIZE. EXECUTE

mediocrity or anything less than what you believe. Once you allow yourself to adapt to the opinions of others, you will mentally quit on yourself. You will begin to use their opinions as garments to clothe your belief system. As a result, you will always look to others to validate you, your dream, and your performance.

Protect your why at all costs. This obstacle will certainly stunt your growth. Many people have conditioned themselves to allow the negative narrative to take residence in their minds and hearts. Unfortunately, they succumb to it and accept the words of those who do not even believe in them or desire to see them prosper. They are barely hanging on with the lack of belief and vision for themselves. How can they attempt to advise anyone else? Have you identified who is genuinely in your corner? Have you identified those who are qualified to speak into your life and give you sound advice? If not, people can take your emotions on a ride that you did not expect. Properly evaluate who is for you and who is against you before you consider adjusting your journey.

You will find yourself second-guessing or going back to the drawing board. You would begin to place your dreams and goals on the backburner or discontinue your efforts for it. This results from you improperly deciphering or discerning if this person is credible to give

DREAM. IDENTIFY. VISUALIZE. EXECUTE

any advice. For example, your dream or goal is to purchase a home. You have saved up the money for the down payment, researched the neighborhood you are considering, and ready to purchase. You may encounter someone that will tell you all the negatives about purchasing a home, such as being responsible for maintenance, taxes, or home insurance. They will give you every reason not to buy it. The catch is, they have never personally owned a home.

On the other hand, someone who currently owns a home will tell you all the purchasing benefits. At this moment, you should evaluate and decide who is qualified to give you sound advice and direction. If someone lacks assets and gives advice, how is this beneficial to you? Where is the evidence? Where is the personal experience to truly help others? Yes, you can advise people from a place of research or what others have experienced. In most cases, I rather hear advice from someone that has experienced the journey. I can learn and gain wisdom at that moment.

Throughout the journey, many find themselves moving but not praying. You begin to listen to everyone but the One who gives you wisdom. Through prayer, you are able to gain wisdom and understanding for everything in your life. With prayer, you would become more encouraged to

DREAM. IDENTIFY. VISUALIZE. EXECUTE

pursue and self-invest. It is a strategy all by itself. Why would you not consider prayer as a part of your strategic plan to accomplish your dreams and goals? Regardless of what you desire to do or be and what strategy you decide to choose; prayer is always essential!

WHO IS THE MOUNTAIN?

The mountains in your life can have two different narratives. From one perspective, mountains could be a huge blockage or an unachievable level. Many people can identify people, places, or things as mountains in their lives. When people think of these things, the feeling of defeat overwhelms them. They make the decision not to do the climb to conquer their mountain. While negative mental activity is taking place, everything you desire is buried or set aside.

This allows mediocrity to step in to take residence. At this point, it is easier to give up and less painful than attempting the climb. From another perspective, a mountain can be a victory ground or a strength builder. From this perspective, after you have endured the climb, the top becomes the place of accomplishment. Many will look at the mountain and become inspired to climb. They do not accept defeat and become motivated by the challenge to conquer it. Yes, it may present itself to be intimidating. However, the one who has faith and drive will accept the challenge to defeat what intimidates others. Their mindset is that defeat is never an option. Although you may get bruises, cuts, and encounter pain you have never experienced before, take the climb! No matter what the situation may be, take the climb!

Climbing is sweat equity, which requires work and energy. It empowers you yet challenges you. For those who would hate to put in the work, are you saying you do not have the energy to see your life endeavors come to past? Put in the effort according to your ability. What is sweat equity? It is long nights spent in your office or creative space, cleaning and clearing things that can hinder your future success, consistently pushing yourself to pursue your dreams and goals, or reading books to enhance your wisdom and knowledge. All of this will help you form and create what you desire in life. It will yield self-gratification and a great sense of accomplishment.

For those who decided to move in faith and endure the journey, you will not regret it! While you are on the quest for your dreams and goals, you will be able to identify your level of strength and courage. While you are striving to push, this is not the time to have lazy, poor mentality people around. You can recognize these people based

DREAM. IDENTIFY. VISUALIZE. EXECUTE

upon the type of energy that they bring. We would categorize anyone or anything that is against our vision as a mountain itself. It is hard enough trying to climb and take on the mountains that naturally come our way.

Do they really think you need any negativity added to the challenge? You don't need any extra weights, baggage, or challenges to weigh you down. This one is for your dreams and goals! Tell yourself, "I am removing what is holding me back and I am pushing to pursue." However, there is another level to this. Think about it. What if it is you that is the mountain? Now, let us talk about it! What happens when you are causing the hindrance or hold up? Stop spending time blaming everything and everyone for you not accomplishing your dreams or goals. You must evaluate if it is a self-inflicting issue or deriving from something or someone else? Be honest with yourself because the more excuses you create, the longer it will take for you to reach your desired results. You must be real with yourself, take responsibility to progress, and reset!

Once you have identified what is preventing you from forward progression, make the adjustments. If it is you, **move out of your own way**! Keep in mind, as you confront yourself, be prepared for the fight. Nothing great will come unchallenged! The what-ifs, what-abouts, and why

DREAM. IDENTIFY. VISUALIZE. EXECUTE

me's will make you question yourself and settle with excuses. **Let nothing stop you from moving!** In these moments, you have to remember where you are headed and fight through the difficulties. The fight will be worth it!

Whether it is you or not, do not become imprisoned in your current situation or your past! Push through it; conquer your thoughts and the opinion of others. Challenges are not meant to take you out; they are meant to take you up. Use those opportunities to elevate you, not deviate you. Having the "do not quit" or "I am not quitting" mentality will yield an incredible harvest in your life if you persevere through it all. The more you push, the more you will achieve. The harder they fight, the greater the reward. What will you choose? Only you can make that decision. Will you stand in your own way, or will you stand on your why?

IDENTIFY GENERATIONAL CYCLES

Another viewpoint in this phase is to identify the challenges that your family has faced. This will attack the obstacles to break the generational cycles. What are generational cycles? They are unbroken habits and mentalities that carry from one generation to the next.

DREAM. IDENTIFY. VISUALIZE. EXECUTE

If someone doesn't recognize them and avoid the habits or mentality, then the cycle repeats itself. Recognizing and attacking generational habits, behavioral patterns, and cycles can be a roadmap to your success. If your family struggled financially, make it your duty to educate yourself in financial literacy. Educating yourself helps to prevent you from making the same pitfall that your predecessors made.

Unfortunately, the cycle is deeply rooted within your spirit. By default, you will begin to move towards that same path. You have to make up in your mind to break those patterns. If no one in your family has owned a home, that could form a cycle. If your family has a poverty mindset, anger, or addiction problems, that is a cycle. No matter how big or small it is, you must change the narrative. Never compromise with it. Allowing yourself to negotiate, you will realize that you have squandered your life, failing at your family's same failures. Understand that when you decide to disrupt and break a pattern in your life, something will begin to alter. You will feel like you don't fit in.

Wake up, stand up, fight back, and declare that you will break every negative thing in your lineage. The disruption and breaking of a cycle must begin with someone. Who will be the Moses in your family? Why not you? I decree

DREAM. IDENTIFY. VISUALIZE. EXECUTE

and declare, today, you are the Moses of your family. This is your exodus! This is your departure! You are exiting a life of defeat, poverty, unacceptance, and low self-esteem. The cycle you are facing; **this is your exodus**. Move towards the promised land and live the life you desire. I declare you will disrupt and break it. Liberty is your new normal.

YOUR SUBCONSCIOUS HEALTH

You must uncover and self-expose what is in your mind to remove the clutter. This allows you to reach your dreams and goals with a clear path mentally. There are two different levels to our minds, which are our conscious and subconscious mind. With you diving into the two levels, it will allow you to experience a creative breakthrough. Our consciousness is the surface level. It allows us to set the atmosphere and get things completed. It is something that we can depict firsthand. Our subconscious mind stores our thoughts, visions, and possibilities to allow us to dream. How many in the world need to dig deeper?

The goal is to break through the surface level. I believe many are in need of an increase in their press and pursuit to reach their subconscious mind. If you could overcome

DREAM. IDENTIFY. VISUALIZE. EXECUTE

the obstacle in your mind, you would gain access to more. Many are ready to work, dream, and write out goals without a vision. What is the vision for your future? While you are on the journey to achieving your dreams and goals, your mental health plays a significant role in accomplishing them. While your conscious mind and physical bodies are at rest, your subconscious mind is at work. It is the reason why you can visualize. You must strengthen and improve both levels of your mind. You can do this by considering your environment and association, what you read, how you see things, daily reminders of your why, and what you desire. The way you train your conscious and subconscious mind for success is vital. The more your train, the more you will attain!

Likened to the diver, the more they train their mind to win, the better chance they have at winning an Olympic medal. Do you have a healthy conscience level? What training mechanisms do you currently have in place that will continue to feed your conscious and subconscious mind to win? These questions are essential to have an answer. Your conscious and subconscious mind will bring awareness and help you self-critique the way you process success. They will also bring direction on how to seek out new information and engage in growing mentally before you can grow physically. Understand you must grow from your past failures and thought patterns. If the way you

DREAM. IDENTIFY. VISUALIZE. EXECUTE

did things were ineffective and did not produce the success you desire to see, a change must occur.

Mental cycles are hard to break. Due to you programming and conditioning your mind, it will function a certain way when change initiates. This is where the difficulty resides. This is when the battle initiates. Your mind will create a million reasons why you should remain in the same place that you are in. However, the necessary changes can take place if you are intentional at creating better habits. You must break your patterns to create and manage what you are trying to accomplish. Studies show, it takes approximately 18 plus days to break it and create a new one. The more intense and disciplined you are, the faster the habit is broken to prevent a new one to be created.

An effective way to battle the mental fight of breaking cycles or habits is to break the norm. You must be willing to sacrifice and endure the process. It can have a stronghold on many people. For some, it has conditioned their conscious and subconscious mind. You must become and remain intentional about what you need to do to change. Write it out and strategize. Stop trying to change what has conditioned you without a thought-out plan. "JUST D.I.V.E" comes with a plan and an effective way to strategize. It is not a strategy to only speak what

DREAM. IDENTIFY. VISUALIZE. EXECUTE

you desire, and it shall happen. It is more to the process! Some people have a vision but lack execution, while others have execution and no vision!

Habakkuk 2:2 says, "Write the vision; make it plain on tablets, so he may run who reads it." Being reminded of your dream keeps you energized and focused. It is great to hear and see it multiple times a day. The more you read your **written** dream out loud to yourself, the more it gives you the passion for accomplishing it. This will begin to train the conscious and subconscious mind to search out new information, attract and recognize ways to succeed, and accomplish a small piece of the total dream on a daily level.

Write down every thought, emotion, or new idea that comes to you while pursuing your purpose, dreams, and goals. Allow yourself to feel the emotions behind reading and running with your vision. It will supply the fuel you need to succeed. Your subconscious mind will give you alerts when things are not in alignment. Do not ignore the alerts given because you will fall back into the same cycle you have previously broken. Stay connected and in-tune with your dreams and vision to make the necessary changes for forward progression.

I am concerned and alarmed with the "fake it until you make it" method. Your mind could quickly become

DREAM. IDENTIFY. VISUALIZE. EXECUTE

adapted to faking success until your dreams and goals become stagnated and foreign. It is not healthy for your subconscious mind. It leads you to become addicted to false success and efforts. For example, I'll use someone posing on social media for attention. This individual will become so consumed with finding the next pose to post until true success becomes distant. At this point, your habits to become successful are vain and shallow. This will cause you to be socially rich and physically, mentally, emotionally, and financially poor.

Never measure success by how many social media likes and hearts you receive. The moment you stop receiving them, your mind will process this as a failure. In actuality, your mind will process this failure before initiating the journey to success. If you would like to take everyone on your journey via social media, I would advise you to plan and take action to accomplish your dreams and goals. Show them what you are doing in the process. Show them what you are executing. Doing this will create momentum that will drive you right into your destination.

DISCOVER YOUR STRENGTHS

Identifying and understanding your strengths are vital. This will be the foundation for your dreams and goals.

DREAM. IDENTIFY. VISUALIZE. EXECUTE

Typically, people do not start a business, chase careers, or start initiatives in areas they lack strength or wisdom. That is illogical and unsound. Successful people build on their strengths and work on their weaknesses to become stronger. For example, if someone is extroverted, then relating to people and building relationships will quickly come. It is more like second nature to them. You must understand your strengths to help you become more calculating and strategic. Knowing what you are good at will allow you to move with confidence and precision.

It will enable you to recollect past victories to cultivate and develop your vital areas for success. Take a minute to think about what you are good at doing? What do you find comfortable and second nature to you? What makes you different and unique from others? For instance, if I were to mention Michael Phelps, you would think of swimming. With Steve Jobs, you would think of Apple. If I were to mention Serena Williams, you would think of tennis. With First Lady Michelle Obama, you would think of leadership and empowerment. What comes to mind when people mention your name?

Knowing what makes you different will be the compass to the success of your future. Once you have discovered your strengths, focus on being successful with your identified talent, gift, and ability. Think of ways to

DREAM. IDENTIFY. VISUALIZE. EXECUTE

separate yourself from the crowd to be unique and different. Think about how people could benefit from your strength, talent, gift, or ability. What problem can your uniqueness solve? The more valuable the solution to the problem is, the more valuable and successful you become. For example, Thomas Edison solved the problem with sustained darkness by inventing the light bulb. David, in the Bible, solved the problem of the Israelites by defeating the Goliath. With your strengths being the focal point, innovative ideas will begin to flow. Find an area that needs a solution, whether corporate, entrepreneurial, ministry, or retail. Submerge yourself in your strengths and watch the possibilities become available and yield unbelievable results.

Another strength to draw from that many undervalue is our social circle. Sometimes, our direct sphere of influence can be our lifeline. The individuals you associate with can help you develop and cultivate new strengths or cause you to abandon everything. I cannot stress enough how vital your sphere of influence is to you. It is a saying that says, "If you hang around four broke friends, you will become the fifth." That statement is also true in reverse, "If you hang around four wealthy friends, you will become the fifth."

DREAM. IDENTIFY. VISUALIZE. EXECUTE

People who have access to speak into your life will always pull you in their direction or environment. If your social circle leads to greater, they will pull you into greater. This is where their attention and focus will always be. In the same light, if your social circle is mediocre and complacent, they will pull you into mediocrity and complacency. This is where their attention and focus will always be, not pushing for greater. You cannot submerge yourself around successful people and never elevate to greater.

The way you view situations, life, and decisions will drastically change. If you are not where you desire to be or headed in that direction, I highly recommend evaluating your social circle. Upgrade to a sphere of influence that will push you. They should be a source of inspiration. Understand good friends will not allow you to fail. They will hold you accountable for your dreams and goals. They will not allow you to make excuses and take shortcuts. If you are the smartest or most intelligent person in your circle, it is time to expand your circle of influence.

Never become the only one who pours out new ideas, wisdom, and knowledge. Your social circle's intellect should be beyond yourself to pour out a wealth of information. This should help you with your dreams and

DREAM. IDENTIFY. VISUALIZE. EXECUTE

goals. Get out of your comfort zone, be okay with becoming uncomfortable, and start networking with people who can influence your life to the next level. Remember, whatever you need can be within or beyond your circle.

DREAM. IDENTIFY. VISUALIZE. EXECUTE

IDENTIFY BIBLICAL INSPIRATION

The story of David defeating Goliath **1 Samuel 17:1-54**

I will present all four stages of **D.I.V.E** within David and Goliath's battle and how David achieved victory. In this chapter of the book, I will show you the **I(dentify)** aspect of David before he fought.

In continuance of the story, after David understood the reward for killing Goliath, he began to internalize defeating the Goliath. With his display of boldness, courage, and strength towards the Goliath, the word got back to King Saul. He became aware that David requested to fight the Goliath. Saul then summoned David to speak with him. Although others may be afraid to take a chance, it does not mean that you have to identify with it. Your boldness will begin to attract people's attention in high places to help fuel your dreams and goals.

Now, as David spoke with Saul, this is where the (I)identification process takes place. David said to Saul, "Let no one lose heart on account of this Philistine; your servant will go and fight him." Saul replied, "You are not able to go against this Philistine and fight him; you are only a young man. He has been a warrior from his youth." David replied to Saul, "Your servant has been keeping his father's sheep. When a lion or bear came to carry off a

DREAM. IDENTIFY. VISUALIZE. EXECUTE

sheep from the flock, I went after it, struck it, and rescued the sheep from its mouth.

When it turned on me, I seized it by its hair, struck it, and killed it. Your servant has killed both the lion and bear. This uncircumcised Philistine will be like one of them. He has defied the armies of the living God. The Lord, who rescued me from the paw of the lion and bear, will rescue me from the hand of this Philistine." Saul said to David, "Go, and the Lord be with you." Then Saul dressed David in his tunic. He put a coat of armor on him and a bronze helmet on his head. David secured his sword over the tunic and tried walking around. He wanted to become acquainted with it.

The other soldiers identified that David was special. Whenever you burn bridges and close doors to prevent from going back, this is where your dreams and goals become a priority. When others are afraid to chase their dreams and goals, they will point out your shortcomings. They pointed out David's flaws, but he knew his abilities. They told David that he was too small and inexperienced for battle. However, David's posture and position was unbothered and perhaps fueled him with more passion. When you have naysayers lining up to express why you cannot achieve success, you need to put on the blinders and eliminate the distractions. As David verbalized to the

DREAM. IDENTIFY. VISUALIZE. EXECUTE

king of his past victories and success, Saul grew to believe in him. Remind yourself of your achievements to gain confidence and determination. You must remind yourself of what God has placed inside of you. Therefore, you can defeat anything that comes against you.

David used the power of affirmation to synchronize his heart and mind to ensure they were on the **same frequency**. He stated if he could defeat a lion and bear from devouring his father's sheep, who is this Philistine? In the same mindset as David, who is fear? Who is defeat? Who are the naysayers? If you can relate to this, speak to yourself and say: I overcame some of the biggest battles of my life, and I will continue to have the victory. You are brave, confident, and fearless. Success will be your portion!

David broke the generational cycle of fear in his family. David's older brothers were fearful to fight in the army. They tried to blanket their fear and insecurities onto David. When they saw David mentally rejecting it and becoming stronger, they became more upset. Many can relate to this! When you are in the process of disrupting and breaking generational cycles, your family and friends will attempt to discourage you with their fear. They would give you the worst-case scenarios of challenges if they knew you were pursuing your dreams and goals.

DREAM. IDENTIFY. VISUALIZE. EXECUTE

Do not allow anyone to put things on you that you are not familiar with. David was never identified with a defeated mindset because he was used to winning. Nor did he fight with armor and swords. Just as David became unaccustomed with defeat and feeling less than, you must break away the commonality to every negative thing. Pursue with authority! The king gave David amour to defend himself in battle; however, David was not used to fighting with it. Do not allow others' strength and strategy to alter your uniqueness or how God told you to do something. Use your slingshot and go for it! "**JUST D.I.V.E.**"

DREAM. IDENTIFY. VISUALIZE. EXECUTE

KEY POINTS

- Clearly define and identify your why.

- Create an atmosphere that supports your why.

- Are you the mountain in your life that is preventing forward momentum?

- Identify the generational cycles in your lineage that could be a problem and find ways to attack them.

- How healthy is your conscious and subconscious mind?

- Eliminate mental cycles.

- Identify what your strengths are and build your future upon them.

- Develop a social circle or sphere of influence that propels you to go after your dreams and goals.

DREAM. IDENTIFY. VISUALIZE. EXECUTE

Take a few minutes to identify and write down the people or things pushing you and preventing you.

_____

_____

_____

_____

_____

_____

_____

_____

_____

_____

_____

_____

_____

_____

_____

_____

_____

_____

_____

_____

_____

_____

_____

DREAM. IDENTIFY. VISUALIZE. EXECUTE

VISUALIZE

— EXECUTION —

Now faith is confidence in what we hope for and assurance about what we do not see. **Hebrews 11:1**

"Never let what your eyes see overpower what your faith sees!" ~**Dennis Carter**

IT'S MORE TO IT

Transitioning from the Take-off (Identify) phase, we are now entering "Execution (Vision)." This is the carrying out of the dive. In this part of the journey, the diver is ready to complete the performance. Before doing any flips, twists, or bends, the diver **visualizes** perfecting the techniques. Your mind will display pictures, little movies, and snapshots of you accomplishing what you desire to do. Once you have the image, you are unstoppable. During the performance, the diver looks to exhibit the proper technique and grace as they glide into the water. The execution must be controlled and held long enough for the judges to recognize the components.

In this phase of the **"JUST D.I.V.E"** strategy, we will discuss the **visualizing** process of your purpose, dreams, and goals. As a dreamer, you will do the same as the diver. You will explore ways to achieve using wisdom, passion, and determination. You must continue building resilience to go after what you want. Develop a great measure of belief to carry out your journey. Having confidence gets you started. The more you are one with the process, the more you will build your belief level. Do you see your potential and the greatness that is within you? Do you know you have what it takes? Do you feel you can effectively execute to reach your destination?

DREAM. IDENTIFY. VISUALIZE. EXECUTE

The way we initiate and follow-through is critical. If you do it incorrectly, you could face the possibility of failing, quitting, or starting over.

The beginning of every new year is an expected time to create vision boards and new year's resolutions. It is a worldwide mission that is very effective if you use it properly. The great thing about this popular activity is that you can initiate the plan and process at any time of the year. If it was any other month, you do not have to wait until the new year to start. No more excuses! Do not allow anything or anyone to prevent you from initiating your new journey. Imagine if you had to wait all year for the month of January to begin your new goals? You would live a limited and delayed life. So, what is a vision board?

It is a visualization tool that refers to building a collage of words and pictures representing the things people desire. I want to paint a short narrative. You receive an invitation to a vision board party for January 2nd. You become excited and meet your friends for a great conversation. You begin the process of creating vision boards with motivation. On February 1st, you find yourself lacking the fire, willpower, ambition, and inspiration you had at the party. You are no longer eager and begin to fall off course. What happened? Well, don't

DREAM. IDENTIFY. VISUALIZE. EXECUTE

feel bad about it! We can all relate to this! How do you change the narrative? You must realize that vision boards go beyond collages, pictures, and great conversation. Do not become so focused on the excitement of vision boards yet lack the vision to accomplish it.

What is the importance of visualizing? It gives you the ability to create the narrative and end-result in your mind. You can envision how you did it and how it made you feel. If you desire a new home, have you ever pictured yourself signing the closing documents? I am sure you saw yourself having family gatherings and creating memorable moments. Or, what about those who are planning a new business? You visualized yourself finding a great location and marketing your business. You envision your clientele and you being successful. Visualizing yourself winning and obtaining what you desire increases your faith and motivation.

When you foresee the journey, you become more inspired and innovative to accomplish every purpose, dream, and goal. This gives you hope and empowers you to keep going. No matter what you want to do, take a moment to imagine how it could be. See yourself becoming it and doing it! Painting the picture is a motivating factor to execute and follow-through.

DREAM. IDENTIFY. VISUALIZE. EXECUTE

Take a moment to do this exercise:

- Go to a quiet, peaceful place to think. Relax your mind and remove the clutter. Many people have an excessive level of mental clutter. How can you effectively visualize with your mental space occupied? Once you remove the clutter, think of what you desire to do or become.
- Begin to reflect and journalize it. What do you see and feel?
- Use this moment to pray about it. Seek God and write the vision He gives you.
- Begin to create your vision board. As you are making it, stay connected to your vision.

Your mind creates pictures for you to remain focused on where you are heading. If you fail to develop current images, then your mind will utilize your past. It will result in you yielding the same outcome as you previously encountered. When this takes place, cycles will form. For example, if you are trying to lose weight. Your mind needs new pictures and information. If you do not provide new visual goals, your mind will not see what you desire to look like or wear. Your old habits will regain control because your mind will remember the pictures of the past. It doesn't have anything new to reintroduce the vision and to keep you on track. These moments are favorable for the hard times. When your old habits arise to derail you from reaching your destination, go back to

DREAM. IDENTIFY. VISUALIZE. EXECUTE

your vision board and see what you visualized. Your why and other motivating factors will begin to kick start your journey again.

Does it mean that you will automatically become closer to your goals? Unfortunately, I can have a vision from God and still become stuck in my process. I can visualize myself losing weight and remain stuck in my habits. I can desire to purchase a home yet continue to lack money management. If you have a vision or can visualize, it is a start. You must take a moment to reflect and remove the clutter. You have the power to dream big and become empowered. However, this does not initially bring immediate results. You can dream, identify, visualize, and still refuse to execute the necessary steps. It cannot work that way. If you are committed to the process, the process will be committed to you.

WHERE IS THE VISION?

The great Helen Keller was an American author and activist for disability rights and politics. Unfortunately, she had an illness at the age of two that left her blind. With this unfortunate event, it is easy to play the victim and develop a defeated mindset. However, she never allowed her blindness to prevent her from having vision. Helen Keller said, "The only thing worse than being blind is having sight but no vision." This statement was so profound and reflective! This statement causes you to

DREAM. IDENTIFY. VISUALIZE. EXECUTE

stop and think about it. Do you have the ability to see, but you are not utilizing the gift to visualize? Your sight would only get you so far. You need vision! Many people are living life just existing. They lack imagination, drive, and passion. How can a person with a vision disability accomplish more than most with the ability to see? It is simple, vision!

The Bible says in **Proverbs 29:18**, "Where there is no vision, the people perish: but he that keepeth the law, happy is he." When you cannot visualize and see beyond your current state, anything and everything you desire will perish. It will wither away and die! At that point, you are merely wishing. You are hoping that you strike luck and life changes for you. However, there is good news! You can change your life. This is merely by exercising the ability to see with your eyes closed. See beyond your eyes! That is called "Faith." "The substance of things hoped for, the evidence of things not seen," says **Hebrews 11:1**. If you have the substance to see what you cannot physically see, soon, you will possess what you saw with your eyes closed.

If you learn how to walk by faith and not by sight, then you will be flowing and operating in the vein of greatness. When your vision aligns with God's will for your life, there is nothing that you cannot accomplish. Everything will line up and harmonize. The question is, do you see what God sees for your life? If not, then you are thinking and visualizing too small. Don't second guess your ability because you feel that you cannot achieve it. What you

DREAM. IDENTIFY. VISUALIZE. EXECUTE

see, God sees more! What you can do, God can do bigger! He can do the impossible! What you think is a mountain, He will give you the strength to either move it or climb it. God said in His word, speak to it, and it will be removed!

Depending on God and putting your trust in Him are two of the greatest things you could ever do! He will always lead and guide you. God has given you divine strength to make it through only if you can see and believe it! Keep believing in yourself. "You can do all things through Christ that strengthens you," says **Philippians 4:13.** It is a reminder of Who gives us strength and the ability to do. By the time you look up, the mountain will be behind you; and your destiny will be one step closer!

PATIENCE WHILE VISUALIZING

Every dream and goal needs time to mature. Having the patience for the manifestation of your vision is going to be a challenge. While pursuing your dreams and goals, you may feel you should have already reached your destination. When you don't meet the deadline of your dreams and goals, you can become discouraged and feel you are on the wrong path. However, can I encourage you that there's power in your patience? There is a process to get to manifestation.

DREAM. IDENTIFY. VISUALIZE. EXECUTE

The Bible says in **Habakkuk 2:3**, "For the vision is yet for an appointed time; but at the end, it will speak, and it will not lie. Though it tarries, wait for it. It will surely come; it will not tarry." Based upon this verse, it suggests that your vision has an appointment. The moment you declare your vision, God takes it and puts a date of manifestation on it. It can be sooner than you expect or later than you planned. Nevertheless, **wait** for it. Yes, I understand you feel like throwing in the towel and quitting. I know your resources are running low. **Wait!** I understand your emotions are racing. **Wait!** Though it tarries, **Wait for it!** Watch this. When it finally arrives, it will not linger. This means it will be everything you imagined and more. It will arrive at the perfect time.

For example, if you booked a flight to reach a destination. You reach the airport, checked in your luggage, and arrived at your boarding gate. While waiting to get on the plane, you hear someone politely inform everyone that there will be a slight delay. Yes, everyone will become upset. You are expected to arrive at your destination at a specific time. While everyone is waiting for the flight to come, no one immediately cancels their flight to return home. They wait! Once the flight is ready to board, everyone is mentally relieved. They understand taking-off is soon. Why can't we have the same patience for our dreams and goals? Regardless of the situation or the challenges, we would still have to wait. Don't become so anxious.

DREAM. IDENTIFY. VISUALIZE. EXECUTE

There is value in your ability to wait. You will begin to learn things along the way and gain understanding. During the process, your mind will develop and mature. Sometimes, the greater the dream, the longer the wait. You have to mentally be ready to embrace the totality of what you have been desiring. You will have to take on new responsibilities and manage them. You must become a steward of your life. For example, you want to become a millionaire, but you have bad spending habits. You fail every month to save what you put in place to save. The million dollars will do nothing but magnify your irresponsibility. It will dig you into a deeper hole of debt because you have not mastered financial management. With time, you will learn the principles of discipline and management. You will begin to retain and grow in every area.

The premature birthing of anything yields a higher risk of complications and birth defects. Many of the main elements in the early stages to sustain a life span are still in need of development. This applies to your purpose, dreams, and goals. You desire for them to yield a mature manifestation. While waiting for the main components to develop, allow yourself time to mature. God knows the perfect time of manifestation. Jesus spoke about patience. He said, "You do not realize now what I am doing, but later you will understand."

One can have a strong passion and desire but lack maturity. Having the absence of developing mentally, emotionally, financially, or spiritually will cause you to

DREAM. IDENTIFY. VISUALIZE. EXECUTE

make premature decisions. The process is not always easy. Sometimes, God uses our waiting period to strengthen and build us for what is to come. While you are waiting for the manifestation of your purpose, dreams, and goals to manifest, you should start self-investing. One way to give back to yourself is by using your time productively and reading to expand your mindset. When the vision comes to past, you want to be able to enjoy the benefits of waiting. Watch the lifespan of your vision sustain for years to come. If you endure the wait, the results of what you desire will be monumental in your life. With hard work and dedication, you will see a fully matured vision come to past. Say to yourself, "**It will be worth the wait!**"

DREAM. IDENTIFY. VISUALIZE. EXECUTE

VISUALIZE BIBLICAL INSPIRATION

The story of David defeating Goliath. **1 Samuel 17:1-54**

I will present all four stages of **D.I.V.E.** within David and Goliath's battle and how David achieved victory. This chapter of the book will show you the **V(isualize)** aspect of David before he fought Goliath.

David is leaving the presence of the king. He took his staff in his hand. Then, he chose five smooth stones from the brook and placed them in the pouch of a shepherd's bag. He then put the sling in his hand. David was ready for battle and drew near to the giant. The Philistine came and began to draw closer to him. The man who bore the shield went before him. When the Philistine saw David, he disdained him.

David was only a youth, ruddy, and good-looking boy. The Philistine said to him, "Am I a dog, that you come to me with sticks?" The Philistine cursed David by his gods. He continued, "come to me, and I will give your flesh to the birds of the air and the beasts of the field!" David boldly said to the giant, "You come to me with a sword, with a spear, and with a javelin. Nevertheless, I come to you in the name of the LORD of hosts. The God of the armies of Israel, whom you have defied.

This day, the LORD will deliver you into my hand. I will strike you and take your head. I will give the camp of the

DREAM. IDENTIFY. VISUALIZE. EXECUTE

Philistines the carcasses to the birds of the air and the wild beasts of the earth. That all the earth may know that there is a God in Israel. Then all who assemble shall know, the Lord does not save with sword and spear. For the battle is the Lord's, and He will give you into our hands."

As David began to make his way to Goliath, he began to visualize himself winning. He picked up the tools that made him feel comfortable for battle. You must understand that this is the fight of your life. You need to choose weapons that you are comfortable with that brought you past victories. See yourself defeating anything that stands in the way of your destiny, like David. Understand that fear has no room to manifest itself while you are visualizing. You are victorious; no matter what anyone says or does, **you are a winner**!

Did you know that you are one decision away from your next level? David needed a Goliath in his life to upgrade him. When you see a giant in your life, this is an indication that your season of promotion is approaching. Press in order to win and soar in your life. Goliath tried to insult and scare David with threats. However, defeating him was his main focus. Do not listen to the enemy. He will try to scare you out of your purpose, desire, and goals. Consume your heart and mind on winning.

No longer will you forfeit your heart's desire due to fear, naysayers, and dream stealers. No longer will you throw in the towel because you don't have the support of others. Sometimes, you don't need support; you need a

DREAM. IDENTIFY. VISUALIZE. EXECUTE

flashback. You need a flashback of every victory in your life. This will give you the reminder and boldness to stand up against any giant that tries to stop you. Just as David said to Goliath, "this day, the **Lord** will deliver you into my hand. I will strike you and take your head." Declare this over your life **today.** The Lord will deliver every negative thing that tries to cause a standstill of your forward progression. You are about to sever the head of poverty, low self-esteem, discouragement, oppression, and depression.

Get up and fight for your dreams and goals. Stop shutting down the dreamer within yourself! Yes, I know that your family does not believe in your purpose, dreams, and goals. **Fight on!** Yes, I know you don't have everything you need to get started! Come on, dreamer! Close your eyes and start visualizing yourself winning and succeeding. Make a self-declaration that in this season of your life, you will walk with your eyes closed. Put your faith in full operation and allow it to mobilize you through it. You are a champion. **"JUST D.I.V.E!"**

DREAM. IDENTIFY. VISUALIZE. EXECUTE

KEY POINTS:

- Visualizing yourself winning and succeeding increases your faith and motivation.
- Create a vision board with a clear vision.
- Your mind needs pictures to remain focused on where you are heading.
- Align your vision with God's vision.
- Learn how to see with your eyes closed.
- Exercise your faith throughout your journey to success.
- Be patient. There is value in the waiting process.
- The premature birthing of anything yields a higher risk of complications and birth defects.
- You want your dreams and goals to yield a fully mature manifestation.
- Remember, it is worth the wait!

DREAM. IDENTIFY. VISUALIZE. EXECUTE

Take a few minutes to visualize yourself pursuing what you desire. Write down the things that come to mind that bring excitement and motivation.

_____

_____

_____

_____

_____

_____

_____

_____

_____

_____

_____

_____

_____

_____

_____

_____

_____

_____

_____

_____

DREAM. IDENTIFY. VISUALIZE. EXECUTE

EXECUTE

═ ENTRY ═

"But as for you, be strong and do not give up, for your work will be rewarded." **2 Chronicles 15:7**

"You do not have to be great to start, but you have to start to be great." **~Zig Ziglar**

DREAM. IDENTIFY. VISUALIZE. EXECUTE

READY SET GO

The last phase for the diver is called Entry (Execute). This is the point where you would make contact with the water. It can be approached by feet or headfirst. It is ideal for entering the water with the body vertically straight. The feet should be together, and the toes pointed. The least amount of splash created, the better the entry will be.

In concluding the **"JUST D.I.V.E"** strategy, let us spend some time on the execution. Likened of the diver, this phase of your journey is significant for the dreamer. This is your official launch and take-off after you have "dreamed, identified, and visualized." You want to ensure you jump headfirst into your purpose, dreams, and goals with precision. Your entire plan should be planned out and organized. The more precise you are, the greater the results you will create. You want to decrease the noise while you are pursuing this mission. You don't want to cannonball or belly flop over the plans you have made. This will create a mess and cause frustration. You need to confirm everything is in alignment with your vision and fulfill it with focus, wisdom, and discipline.

It is time to put all your efforts on paper. Either you are ready to go or still complacent on the shelf! You are

DREAM. IDENTIFY. VISUALIZE. EXECUTE

moving from speaking what you intend to get done to a moment of no excuses and completion. You had a fun time clarifying and classifying your purpose, dreams, and goals. You were able to visualize yourself winning and get in the right mindset. As you remove the clutter, you can make room for the new things that God has for you. Whether it is new information, direction, or provision, you can receive it without any distractions. You should be in a mental space to see it manifest and to become tangible. This is where you take out your pen and paper or technology device. It is time to sit down and strategize **how** to get this done. Your plan must be effective to execute it.

Goal setting is a purposeful process to organize and manage what you desire to achieve. After planning, you need to implement what is in place. It allows you to become challenged, dedicated, and influenced. It allows you to avoid being all over the place and undisciplined. Your execution reflects how bad you want it to come to pass. This allows you to take control of your life. Staying committed to the plan and process will create a smooth, seamless journey.

With preparing and planning, it should give you a sense of accountability and accomplishment. Passion, a strong why, determination, and an effective strategy

DREAM. IDENTIFY. VISUALIZE. EXECUTE

paired with execution yield results. This is an excellent formula for success. The more you deviate from the steps, the harder it will be for you. A plan without execution is a waste of time. Do not allow time to pass you by without daily efforts. Imagine what you can accomplish in a short timeframe. If your purpose, dreams, and goals are significant as you declare, you should have a great determination and commitment level. Don't forget to speak those self-affirmations and write them out.

Make your effort **match** your desire and belief level. You declare you want it and believe in yourself, level up, and do the work! You cannot have this big dream or purpose and lack the work ethic to obtain it! Make a list of your short and long-term goals to remove stress and frustration. How you manage the execution reflects how bad you desire it. You know your goals; let's see if they are realistic and obtainable.

Here are **four** factors to remember when creating your action plan:

1. **Is Your Plan Detailed And Precise?**

    Be sure to define your goals. If you target what you want, you can prepare more effectively and go for it. For example, if I desire to lose weight. Writing down, "I want to lose weight" is not enough information. It is clearer and more defined when

DREAM. IDENTIFY. VISUALIZE. EXECUTE

you write in your journal, "I will lose 60lbs within six months **by** running on a treadmill for one hour, six days a week, and eating healthy. This is detailed and can be measured over time. This action plan tells you exactly how to proceed. Use this as an example to guide you and make it happen!

2. **How Does Each Goal Measure?**

Measuring your goals are great for everything you desire. You may be wondering how to do it? It is simply the process of comparing your starting point to where you desire to be. Your faithfulness to the process will move the hand of God. This should be completed twice a week. Being **intentional** will show you how consistent and dedicated you are. Using a calendar and journaling daily is a great way to measure how you are progressing. If you need to break down your goals and measure them in smaller increments, break your goals down yearly, quarterly, monthly, weekly, or daily.

3. Are Your Goals Reachable?

Validate if your goals are reachable based upon your likeliness of accomplishing them. I know being excited can cause you to exaggerate and be unrealistic. Remember, we are not trying to impress; we are trying to **execute**! Ask yourself, are my goals **attainable**? Are my goals reachable within my stated timeframe? Is it a challenge for me to manage?

Responding to these questions allows you to know how hard you will need to work, your strengths and weaknesses and what is beyond your reach. Plan accordingly.

4. What Is The Appointed Time For Each Goal?

Set an appointed time for your dreams and goals to happen. What is an action plan without a specified time for something to happen? Choose when you will aim to complete it to place a demand on your goals. Furthermore, you are putting a mandate on yourself. Declare, "at this specific time, I will purchase my new home. I will have my new business up and running, and **here is what it takes**." No more sitting on what you desire and shelving your heart's desire. You got this!

IT IS ONLY ONE YOU!

Where you now, you cannot afford to stay in that place. Your dreams are waiting to be released. This release will only happen with your execution. There is more for you to do and to have in this world! Resuscitate those dreams, if needed. Become so focused on implementing your vision until distractions don't matter. Guard your vision and dream board while executing. Do not stop and look at another person's plan or outcome. You will begin to second-guess and compare. This confusion causes many people to alter their thinking and confidence. You would begin to question if what you have is good enough or worthy to pursue. It only creates setbacks and uncertainty. Comparison truly kills! It destroys your spirit, purpose, aspirations, dreams, goals, and vision.

Be content with the capacity level God has graced you with for your life. Commit everything you do to Him so He can establish your plans. **Proverbs 16:3** confirms this to us! Realize that Steve Jobs became great at who he was as an individual and what he could do to make an impact. The same for Martin Luther King, Jr., Warren Buffet, Oprah Winfrey, and many more! Become great with who you are and what you will do to create a legacy

DREAM. IDENTIFY. VISUALIZE. EXECUTE

to be used as an example. Make your commitment level **match** your demand. You want more, pursue more!

Your plan is equally significant and useful. Everyone has a story that connects to their measure of endurance and dedication. Trust the vision God has given you to birth out. He created so much inside of you. Tap into who you are and ignite your fire. You will not always have someone to come and light the match. It is up to you to become consumed and excited. You have a purpose here on earth.

People will never believe in your vision if you don't believe in it. They will question, "why should I invest in you when you can't see the potential or greatness of yourself." Pray and ask God to elevate your belief and confidence. Ask Him to reveal what is preventing you from living it out. Be vulnerable and transparent to say, "God help me to develop the inspiration, faith, discipline, and courage I need to pursue what you have given me."

Another critical factor in executing success is not depending on others and expecting them to see your vision as you see it. We miss the mark living our lives needing the validation of others. Let others figure out what you see in your vision. Show confidence in who you are and what you are doing. Be dedicated and pursue it with excellence. Do not come down from the ladder.

There is work to be done, and it is happening. You cannot come down because it is too costly. Be different, embrace your uniqueness, and trust God in the process for your purpose, dreams, and goals. Build your patience and watch everything flourish in your life. **Winston Churchill** said, "The price of greatness is responsibility." You are responsible for what God placed inside of you. Everything within you is all that it takes to birth your life endeavors and heart's desire. You have a responsibility to birth it out! Too many excuses and options will cause your dreams to die!

THE PASSION TO PURSUE

Fulfill your purpose, dreams, and goals with passion! It will be the driving factor for your vision. Always keep it fresh, fed, and fueled. The more hunger you have, the more momentum you will create. Once you reach a high speed of drive, it produces an offspring called determination. No matter who is for you or who is against you, you would be too determined to quit! The more drive you have that's present, the more willpower you will have to achieve your purpose, dreams, and goals. Feed your passion and increase your faith for faster results. You would reach them in record-breaking timing.

DREAM. IDENTIFY. VISUALIZE. EXECUTE

Never allow anything or anyone to alter or frustrate you. By allowing life circumstances and people to alter your motivation, you are showing others that you can easily be broken or influenced. When you lack passion or inspiration, it is impossible to create sustainable momentum and determination. There is not enough belief in your system to birth anything this way. If you experience the curveballs of life, master them and mobilize back to your purposeful position. Push yourself through the challenging times and execute. The presence and absence of passion both influences and affects your attitude and belief. Always have it in your heart for everything you are pursuing, whether it be for your career, life endeavors, ministry assignments, and many more. Commit to being passionate as you pursue your heart's desire. You never know who you could be inspiring.

EXECUTE WITH TRUTH

Being honest with yourself will only help you. If you can devote a small amount of time towards your purpose, dreams, and goals, I recommend doing it. It will help you develop consistency. If your schedule adjusts and allows more time to pursue them, you should make room to do

DREAM. IDENTIFY. VISUALIZE. EXECUTE

it. Your true efforts will expose themselves in due time. You can claim to do the work; however, you can't falsify the fruit the work produces. No plastic fruit allowed!

Many people are plastic fruit producers because they need to be and feel validated. They love to make public declarations and have high hopes that no one will ever ask to see the results. Why would anyone dare to mention false information to someone who holds them accountable? What happens when you talk more than what you put in? It delays your time of manifestation significantly. There is a difference between affirming and speaking it into existence versus talking. Affirming is backed by belief and actions. Talking is a ball of fluff. You will embarrass yourself and show others that you need validation and not true to yourself. Prayerfully, people will not call you delusional and desperate. Realize that you have nothing to prove to anyone but yourself and God!

Accomplish it with true commitment. Reframe from speeding through your plans. Set and run your own race. Push yourself out of your comfort zone. Don't set laid-back commitments. You will never stretch yourself to become greater. Be truthful and ask, am I pushing myself hard enough? If the answer is no, then apply more pressure. If the answer is yes, ensure you are truly pushing yourself and not just declaring it. We must move from

DREAM. IDENTIFY. VISUALIZE. EXECUTE

what makes us feel comfortable. Being and remaining content is what has many in their current state. Enhance your life to execute with truth and empower yourself to the max.

YOUR MEASURE OF COMMITMENT

What is your level of commitment to your action plan? You should ask yourself every phase along the journey. It is an ongoing process! Every day you should think, "I need to increase my work ethic and keep my head in the game." As you implement, you need to remain committed and dedicated. For manifestation to occur in the appointed season, it will require a new, unfamiliar commitment level. This effort may be a different level, but you can do this. For some, it may seem unfavorable because it is out of their norm. In the end, you will fulfill and experience your heart's desire.

Making sacrifices is a part of what it takes to accomplish what you want. You may have to miss family gatherings, social events, or even delay things you enjoy to keep yourself on track. If anything clashes with your commitment towards what you desire or purposed to do, you need to evaluate it. Many times, people obligate themselves to do more than they can handle. Don't bite

DREAM. IDENTIFY. VISUALIZE. EXECUTE

off more than you can chew. You want to prevent from forming those cycles that have kept you bound and stagnated. **Albert Einstein** once said, "the definition of insanity is doing the same thing over and over again and expecting a different result." No more repeated cycles! No more chains, doors, mountains, or walls to hold you back! **"JUST D.I.V.E!"**

What happens when your dreams and goals demand another level of sacrifice? We spoke about "climbing." I want to paint another picture using that same example. Envision yourself climbing a high mountain. Your dream has always been to get to the top of a mountain. One day, you build the courage to take the climb. You have an amazing start, and you are almost to the median point. Your mind begins to form doubt and fear. You grow tired and need a minute to rest. You start to second guess if you should finish or climb down. Will you allow all of your effort to be in vain? Will you climb this mountain just to celebrate the halfway mark? Yes, you did your best, and you should be proud of your efforts and accomplishment. What if I were to tell you, "you came too far to give up now? What if I told you God would strengthen you in your press to finish the rest?" Moments later, you begin to become encouraged and make it to the top.

DREAM. IDENTIFY. VISUALIZE. EXECUTE

No matter what, stay in the moment! No matter what, finish the climb! The power of commitment can yield your life immeasurable results. Create healthy balances and days of rest. Every push, every sacrifice, every yes is what will sustain you. **If you fail to reach a goal, it does not make you a failure.** Go harder and remain consistent. Let those who are wise in counsel to coach you through the process, if needed. Become a student and maximize every opportunity to learn something new. Many fail because they don't submit to the aspect of learning from someone. Some believe they have it all together and will eventually figure it out. Stop being stubborn and strengthen your work ethic.

I believe you read this book, and you are ready to pursue your dreams, goals, purpose, and vision. No matter how long it takes, it will come to pass! God honors our commitment and faithfulness. In everything you do, become a steward. God will allow you to thrust and thrive into greater. He will open doors for you to thrust and thrive in the things you desire. Many people lack stewardship. Many people want to experience success but fail to be a steward over anything! The biblical view of stewardship is managing and honoring everything that God brings to you. You must strive to be the best manager of your life and what He grants to you. When you do everything honorable and operate in excellence,

God will begin to bless you. God can't bless what you do not honor! Today, I challenge you to become a steward of your purpose, dreams, and goals. Elevate your thinking and faith measure. I hope you are inspired to go forth and produce results. Whether it is a new home, new job, new business, or to attend college, I speak you will make a thought-provoking self-declaration and execute with precision and excellence.

EXECUTE BIBLICAL INSPIRATION

The story of David defeating Goliath   **1 Samuel 17:1-54**

I will present all four stages of **D.I.V.E** within David and Goliath's battle and how David achieved victory. In this chapter of the book, I will show you the **E(xecute)** aspect of David before fighting Goliath.

At the closing of the story, David visualized himself winning the battle. He declared his victory to Goliath. While the Philistine moved closer to attack him, David ran quickly to meet him at the battle line. He reached into his bag to take out a stone and he slung it. The stone struck the Philistine and he fell to the ground. David ended up triumphing over the Philistine because he came in the name of the Lord of Host and the God of the armies of Israel.

David was in the process of performing the execution phase of the **"JUST D.I.V.E"** strategy. He was using his unique fighting style to slay Goliath. He was going forth with precision, focus, and passion. Just as David ran toward the battlefield, you should run to the battle of every Goliath in your life. Show your giant you are not scared. You will not back down. Yes, he was bigger than David, so what? Yes, it seems like your challenges and fears are bigger than what you can handle. You have God on your side to guide you and give you a strategy to win.

Do you realize that you are standing in front of your promise?

Be like David and take out your weapons and strike every mountain, stumbling block, and hindrance in your life. You have the victory! What are your weapons? The Word of God, self-affirmations, determination, faith, consistency, boldness, and this book for motivation. Do not allow anyone or anything to stand in the way of your next level or new season. You have everything you need to succeed. All you have to do is go in your bag! Reach for your joy and peace! Reach for your promise and promotion! Reach for your healing and breakthrough! **REACH!**

I want to make a declaration to you. Every mountain, feeling of oppression, depression, fear, and doubt will be removed. In Jesus' name! I speak to every negative seed that tries to take root in your mind and heart. I declare it shall uproot itself and return to where it belongs. Freedom, success, and victory is your portion! By this time next year, I declare you will see the fruit of your labor. God will allow you to walk into a season of more than enough. This is your moment of breakthrough! Believe it and receive it! **JUST D.I.V.E!**

DREAM. IDENTIFY. VISUALIZE. EXECUTE

KEY POINTS:

- Make sure everything is in alignment with your vision and execute with focus, wisdom, and discipline.

- Ensure that your goals are measurable and realistic.

- Execute your vision with so much focus until everything around you do not matter.

- Passion will be your driving factor. Always keep your passion and vision fresh, fed, and fueled.

- Never allow anything or anyone to alter your thought process or passion for your vision.

- Be truthful to yourself.

- The power of commitment can yield your life immeasurable results.

Take a few minutes to write down your plan of action that you are going utilize to implement for your purpose, dreams, and goals.

_____

_____

_____

_____

_____

_____

_____

_____

_____

_____

_____

_____

_____

_____

_____

_____

_____

_____

_____

DREAM. IDENTIFY. VISUALIZE. EXECUTE

JUST

D.I.V.E

Remove Fear and Shift Your Life from Potential to Greatness

DREAM. IDENTIFY. VISUALIZE. EXECUTE

DREAM. IDENTIFY. VISUALIZE. EXECUTE